TWO TOCKS BEFORE MIDNIGHT

THE AGORA MYSTERY SERIES 1

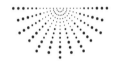

CLAY BOUTWELL

WWW.CLAYBOUTWELL.COM

ISBN 9781973555810

∾

Visit the author's website at http://www.ClayBoutwell.com

FREE EBOOKS

Join Clay Boutwell's Readers First Club for free and get **two FREE eBooks**.

Simply go to www.ClayBoutwell.com and click on "Send me my books" to get a Clay Boutwell starter library absolutely free.

❧

Want the audio book version? Get it for free.

With Audible, you can! Enjoy the audiobook of Two Tocks before Midnight absolutely free when you enter Audible's 30 day free trial. You can cancel at any time.

To get the Audiobook to Two Tocks before Midnight for FREE, follow these steps:

1. Go to the Two Tocks before Midnight Audible page.
2. Click on the "Free with 30 Day Trial" link
3. Enjoy!

Are you already a member?

Check out how to get Two Tocks before Midnight at a reduced price. Simply go here:

https://www.audible.com/pd/Fiction/Two-Tocks-Before-Midnight-Audiobook/B008DVY176/

∾

ALSO BY CLAY BOUTWELL

THE AGORA MYSTERY SERIES

The Agora Letters - For the first time, get the first five stories in the Agora Series in a single volume at a reduced price.

Two Tocks before Midnight - When a flurry of forgeries appear in museums and among collectors, the members of the Agora, a society dedicated to the betterment of man, take it upon themselves to stop the rogues.

The Penitent Thief - A string of thefts ends in a grisly murder. Certain evidence leads Captain Barnwell to suspect a former thief, Rutherford Nordlinger as the culprit. Carl Brooke becomes personally involved as Nordlinger's guilt is questioned.

The Peace Party Massacre - Kidnapped! An honorable man has gone missing and his wife is not in the least helpful. The sheriff dithers and every day brings death closer to a reality.

The Curse of the Mad Sheik - A grieving widow believes her husband's death to be something more than a failing heart. A ruby—

said to be cursed—had been found in his hands. The police and her closest kin say otherwise.

The Captain's Play - Captain Barnwell, long an honorary member of the Agora Society, presents to the members a solved case one clue at a time. Three suspects. One is the murderer.

Murder by Monday - Set in the late 1800s, Carl Brooke and his friend Rutherford Nordlinger are called to the aid of a man who, accused of murder, is now threatened by the man he is said to have killed.

Eggs over Arsenic - An art critic is brutally murdered. The main suspect: the subject of the critic's last review.

THE TEMPORAL SERIES

The Temporal — A devastating earthquake in central Japan sends eternity crashing into time, enabling Sam to hear echoes of the past and even the future. Through the echoes, Sam and a mysterious Japanese woman learn of a terrorist plot that could plunge the world into turmoil and position a murderer as the leader of the free world.

A Temporal Trust — After stopping a terrorist plot to position a murderer as president, Sam Williams must come to grips with his newfound abilities. As one of the Temporal, his encounters with eternity give him both gifts and challenges to overcome as a new threat emerges that could wipe out the Temporal for all time.

Carritos — In 1906, the San Francisco earthquake took everything from Jackson. It took, but it also gave. He soon found he had been given the ability **to...stop time,** to "freeze" the world around him. He lives the good life among tiny mortals. Stealing, bribing, stumbling his way into making a living. All this can be forgiven, he figures, as long as he keeps two rules. Just two, but they are absolute and non-negotiable: *thou shalt not kill and family comes first.* Now

Jackson must make a choice, a choice that will change everything. **The choice is: which rule will he break?**

THE TANAKA SERIES

Tanaka and the Yakuza's Daughter — Akira Tanaka's past as an undercover agent in Tokyo's underworld has caught up with his present. Now he must find out who kidnapped his only daughter, and why. Can he rescue her before it's too late?

CHAPTER ONE

October 24th, 1889
Carl Brooke
Boston

I HAVE NEVER BEEN FOND OF SENTIMENTAL RAMBLINGS SO I will keep this short. Indeed, were it not for the insistence of my friends, I would soon let the matter slip away with the sands of time. But repeated pleas from the curious and the morbid alike compel me to share with you the strange affair of October 24th, 1859.

I cannot say with certitude the events of this date occurred exactly as I remember them. As time passes, so do the minute and myriad details; rough edges are made smooth, and the inevitable romanticizing of the past is liable to play havoc with true fact.

Still, as I am a Christian and an honest man, what follows is as accurate as my fallible mind can relate.

Nearly two score years separate us from those days and that night in particular. I, alone—so I am told—am survived out of the lot of us.

Before I begin to describe the events of that night, I think it important to share a little more about our group.

We were the *Agora Society*, an open marketplace to foster ideas for the betterment of man. That was the aim; the structure, however, was modeled after Dr. Franklin's *Junto Society*. In a show of hubris that even today causes me to shudder with embarrassment, our charter set forth the goal of leaving to the world a greater legacy than that of the good Doctor. Indeed, we had the mind to compete with the man who "took lightning from the sky and the scepter from the tyrant's hand" as Turgot put it. He surely laughs at my friends in the hereafter. I fear there are times when I hear his laughter echoing in my dreams, beckoning for me to come.

I do not think it wrong, however, to recollect our accomplishments—as dim as they may be when held up to Dr. Franklin's light.

During the years of our club's existence, we established a Freeman's society which secured the release of one hundred and thirty-six slaves. We also ensured these men and women were taught a trade and their letters. It is of considerable pride to report nearly all of them transitioned well after the War between the States. Indeed, several families prospered. To this day, I have no greater joy than to receive a letter or a visit from a member of one of these families.

Another source of pride came when the Society financed the repairing of the dam in Clarkesville, which was completed a mere month before the great flood of fifty-six. Over the years, we were involved with building libraries, windmills, schoolhouses, and churches.

It is also true that our services were used on a number of occasions by the police, as this letter will attest. Though small, we were well-connected and able, by merit of our collective talents, to be of some value to law enforcement.

In short, our efforts saved the lives of hundreds of mortal

and immortal souls. However, again remembering our foolish goal, Dr. Franklin's invention of the simple lightning rod alone, has surely saved millions.

Our society, the *Agora Society*, had a dozen members at its zenith. Each brought to the group his individual talents and ambitions. Mine lay in ancient Near Eastern languages.

To give a brief sampling of the others pertinent to our discussion, my dear friend, Dr. Christopher Harding, an expert in papyrus, cuneiform, hieroglyphics, and other writing methods of antiquity, led the initial discussion of the matter; Mr. Thomas Phillips, knowledgeable in ancient warfare and weaponry, could always be heard quoting some obscure Greek or Roman philosopher; and of course, Mr. Charles Tock could converse in thirteen languages and read five more. Charles Tock and Thomas Phillips are of special interest to our story.

The weekly meetings were held every Monday evening at precisely six of the clock. If someone was absent or tardy, he was made to do "community service." This usually meant clearing the streets of horse manure. The delights of such an occupation was a great incentive to arrive on time, and it was a rare occasion when one of us failed to do so.

Charles Tock joined our august group a few years before the events of that dreadful night. I should note, as a matter of protocol, we referred to each other by our first names no matter our age or status outside the *Agora*. I distinctly remember Charles' introduction the first evening he appeared before our group. I relate it now because it accurately illustrates his dry humor and the breadth of his academic knowledge.

"My name is Charles," he said, pausing to allow his eyes to greet each of us. "That can't be helped, but I always intended to marry royalty to avoid being churlish."

Only a few of us caught the etymological jesting. Having a

3

name, Carl, that shares the same cognate as Charles, namely "churl," I was one of them. "Churl," as you know, came to mean the opposite of nobility, a rude man somewhat above a peasant.

Despite his poor taste in arcane humor, Charles' broad knowledge and experience soon propelled him to something of an elder position among us—a natural state of affairs, since the majority of us were more than two decades his junior.

In the years since these events, many people have asked me if we suspected anything unusual about him from the beginning. In retrospect, he could be willing to compromise his principles to achieve his aims. He had demonstrated this vice in small ways over the few years we knew him, but so subtle and inconsequential were these incidents, no one made mention of them in complaint. None of us could have anticipated his spectacular downfall.

He arrived suddenly, and one winter morning, left just as suddenly—and without telling anyone. As I have already attested, missing even a single meeting was heavily discouraged. This transgression was doubly shocking considering how integral he had made himself to the club.

On the third meeting after his extended absence, we decided a party should be sent to learn what had become of him. The talk of discipline from the week before turned to genuine concern. I was not among those chosen to join the search party, but I did receive their report. Charles' lodgings —the address he gave in the society's records—was an abandoned slaughterhouse. As it turned out, no member had visited Charles outside club meetings during the entire time he had been with us. Being a band of honorable men, we took our members word as fact. This trust, unfortunately, allowed opportunity for abusers.

But the mystery had only begun.

Winter turned to spring, and spring to summer. It is difficult to overstate our total and utter amazement when a full six months after his disappearance, Charles Tock quietly walked through the doors of the *Agora Society* once more. Bearded and dirty, he wore a tattered frock coat and carried a lantern that cast a circle of yellow light, illuminating his features. He looked churlish to say the least.

While not against club rules, facial hair was a rarity among us. Only one of us, Thomas Phillips, had a neatly trimmed mustache. The rest of us, during those days, were clean-shaven and therefore seeing Charles with an abundance of facial hair was doubly shocking.

With him stood a large, similarly dressed man in dark clothing carrying a leather case with a large brass buckle.

A hushed pause descended as we all turned and stared at the strange sight.

CHAPTER TWO

PLEASE ALLOW ME TO INDULGE IN A LITTLE NARRATIVE. WHILE the phrasing may be somewhat inaccurate, I shall be as true to my memory as my venerable age allows.

"CHARLES, where the devil have you been?" one of us blurted out.

He walked to the front and set his lantern on the table. His companion remained near the entrance.

"I've been traveling. This is… Joseph," Charles answered while nodding toward the large man to his side. Charles looked as though he had aged ten years. Beads of sweat rolled down his cheeks and into his beard. This was not odd considering the heat of the summer, yet, somehow, the sweat seemed to be of a different sort.

We were in shock, both by Charles' unexpected return after these many months of absence and by the presence of this stranger, a clear violation of the society's charter.

"Charles, there are certain rules with which you must

surely be acquainted," I said, trying to admonish him as lightly as I could.

"Joseph will leave shortly, but he has something that will undoubtedly be of considerable interest to all, and, Carl, to you in particular."

Our interest piqued, the president motioned for Charles to step forward and address the meeting. Charles nodded and moved to the front while patting his forehead with a handkerchief.

"I do apologize for the abrasive nature of my reappearance. It was unavoidable, I'm afraid." He paused to once again pat a fresh bubbling of sweat. It seemed some heaviness hindered him from continuing. Surely hidden from the crowd, but not from me, Joseph move his fist slightly, prompting Charles to continue. "Yes, well, Joseph, please present the document."

The room was quiet save for the striking of a clock and the occasional hawker announcing his wares on the street below. I doubt any of us noticed those things, however. Such was the tense atmosphere.

With rough movements, the stranger pulled a parchment from his case. Even from that distance, the manner in which he handled what seemed to be an ancient document brought a shudder to my frame.

Contrary to club protocol, I pushed through the others to observe the object closer. Dr. Christopher Harding, the expert on papyrus and other ancient writing utensils, was equally inquisitive and also stepped forward.

The scroll was clearly ancient, and the writing, Paleo-Hebrew. The sheepskin had been prepared in the proper way as befitting an ancient Torah scroll. But it most certainly was not a Torah scroll.

"Can you read it, friend?" Joseph grunted, baring his

teeth. The tone, rather than the words, betrayed an aggressive impatience.

My hand trembled as fingers hovered an inch above the precious parchment. Christopher examined the physical document, devoting special interest to the edges and damage wrought by countless years. I, meanwhile, studied the language.

"My word," Christopher said. "Where did you discover this?"

"A dig in the Middle East," Joseph answered before Charles could open his mouth. Neither man elaborated further.

"What is it?" a member asked.

It seemed the entire room refused to breathe until we made known the contents of the parchment.

"It is a... *gevil*," Christopher answered, "written in the Paleo-Hebrew script, but as to the contents, you will have to ask Carl."

Christopher's matter-of-fact response of a *"gevil"* remained unsatisfactory for our fellow members unschooled in ancient writing materials.

I explained. "A *gevil* is a specially prepared animal skin used by Jewish scribes, particularly for Torah scrolls."

"Is it, then, a Torah scroll?" asked one member.

"No."

I wasn't sure what it was, but it was no Torah scroll. Christopher handed me a magnifying glass and backed away, giving me room for the examination. I said nothing for a few minutes and, understanding my need for concentration, no one spoke or made a sound.

"A Bible, please," I asked.

We kept a large Bible on the shelf inside the stand for the initiation ceremony and for occasional reference. It was handed to me and I consulted two places to confirm my memory.

"Most extraordinary." The elation I felt at that moment brought forth a grin to my face I could not contain.

"My dear, Carl," said Christopher, eyes wide and glowing with anticipation. "Please do not keep us in suspense. I shall have to leap from London Bridge if you are not forthright this moment."

"My apologies, Christopher. Based on your experience, how old would you say the parchment may be?"

Christopher cleared his throat before answering. "It would be impossible to know for sure. The quality is unsurpassed. Lesser specimens would still have traces of animal hair. Clearly, this was from a roll and not a codex which would be similar to a modern book. In general that suggests pre-fifth century A.D., but I dare not hazard a more specific guess."

"Would you say... mid-ninth century is possible?" I asked, perhaps a little too playfully.

"Yes, but as I mentioned, as it is from a roll, pre-fifth century is..."

"No, my good man," I said, raising my eyebrow and managing to wipe the smile from my face. "Not A.D. The ninth century B.C."

A hush fell around us as all waited for Christopher to respond. Only the hiss of the two gas lamps on the wall broke the silence.

"Yes," he said, bracing his arms on the table for support. "It is possible. The parchment is in very good shape, but if it had been kept in a dry, cool storage and undisturbed... yes, it is possible. But how can you be so specific?"

"The corner," I said, pointing to the lower left area. "Can you read it?"

The line wouldn't have given pause for someone with even rudimentary Hebrew.

"*Melech*," he said after sounding out the three characters. "*Achazyah... Chai. Melech Achazyah Chai!*" His arms flew up and his eyes danced with excitement. "My dear fellows," he said turning to the other men who had—against all society etiquette—crowded around us with the greatest of curiosity. "King Ahaziah lives! This was written during the reign of the great, great, great, great, great grandson of King David. Mid-ninth century B.C. would be on target."

"The Paleo-Hebrew style is consistent," I said finding it increasingly difficult to withhold my excitement.

"But," spoke up one of the men behind me. "What of its contents?"

I answered promptly. "There is little doubt. I have only had a few minutes to examine it, but if I had to make a judgment this very moment, I would have to say this may well be a segment of the Sefer HaYashar—the Book of Jasher."

I went to explain the Book of Jasher was one of the "lost" books from the biblical period, being named in scripture but no longer extant. When the sun stood still for Joshua, the book is mentioned for further reference. David bade them to teach the sons of Judah the use of the bow as mentioned in this book.

"If memory serves, Josephus said the Hebrews stored the Book of Jasher in the temple nearly two thousand years ago. It was thought lost after the destruction of Jerusalem in seventy A.D.," added someone.

Charles seemed relieved, but somehow unhappy. Joseph smiled as he spoke, "Would you, then, gentlemen, certify its authenticity?" Just as before with "friend," the way he muttered "gentlemen" seemed somehow quite unfriendly.

Thomas Phillips, who had been one of the more excitable among us regarding the parchment, spoke: "It would be our honor, wouldn't it, boys?" His curled mustache wiggled with the words.

I held up a cautious hand. "My good fellow, I would love to—upon further examination, of course. I must study the text in detail and compare it with other so-called '*Books of Jasher*' discovered in the last century.

Joseph's smile dropped and he snatched his lantern from the table. "You have an hour. I shall return to collect the parchment then." With that, Joseph and Charles were gone.

I spent the next few minutes rapt in joy. The others took turns peering over my shoulder or standing in front, occasionally interrupting my examination with their comments —sometimes helpful, sometimes not. It had grown too dark for the wall lamps by that time and two candles were brought near to illuminate the text.

Only after half an hour of study did I discover something that would condemn three souls to their deaths.

CHAPTER THREE

I FELT THE BLOOD DRAIN FROM MY FACE AS I GRIPPED THE EDGE of the table in a vain attempt to steady my nerves.

"What is the matter, Carl?" asked Christopher.

One heavy heartbeat later, I responded. "I... I am afraid there may be a problem."

I pointed to two Hebrew letters and asked Christopher to read them.

"Yes, yes," Christopher replied. "It is the common Hebrew word *'shel.'* It means 'of' or 'belonging to.' What is your point?"

"*'Shel'* is a syntactical innovation of a much later date."

Never have I felt such deep disappointment befall so many people as a result of my words.

"Not only that, Christopher," I said, handing him the magnifying glass. "Look closely at the ink here and here."

Christopher took the glass and bent over the parchment.

"My word. I didn't see it before, but while the parchment does appear to be quite old, the writing seems to be newer. The flaking here," he said, pointing to a tiny area missing some ink, "indicates the ink has not had time to bond. And here, we see a scratch in the parchment running through this aleph and yet the ink is unharmed. Good eye, Carl."

"And," I said, driving the last ounce of doubt from my mind, "if held against the light, one can see nearly invisible pencil marks—very modern pencil marks, undoubtedly a practice run before inking."

We were all, of course, greatly disappointed, but in the end, we agreed the specimen was nothing but a clever fraud. Even Thomas Phillips who had offered the best counter-arguments eventually conceded after facing the over-whelming evidence.

Our name would not be soiled, but we would have to break the news to Charles and Joseph. By their reactions, we expected to determine whether they had foreknowledge of the forgery.

A FEW MINUTES LATER, Joseph returned without Charles.

"Well?"

"I'm afraid," I said, speaking up as the representative of our club, "you have a clever forgery here."

"What do you mean?" Joseph's mouth shut tight and his eyes turned blood-red.

"I mean, the text cannot be but a few months old," I said, returning the carefully rolled parchment to him.

Joseph clenched his fists and then relaxed them, appar-ently thinking better of it. He snatched the parchment and stormed out without a word or a tip of his hat.

CHAPTER FOUR

THE EXCITEMENT PRODUCED BY CHARLES AND JOSEPH FILLED the club with talk the next week, but it was soon forgotten as time passed. We were concerned about Charles of course, but as before, we had no idea where to find him. No one wanted to say it out loud, but we all suspected Charles of having a hand in creating the forgery.

Weeks passed and then months. One day, a member arrived at my door rather agitated. He told me he had been traveling to Chelsea and discovered the very parchment Joseph and Charles had brought. It was on display at a museum—which museum, I will not say out of respect for the director.

We immediately called the others, and the majority instantly decided to make the journey to the museum. Thomas, despite being one of the more excited among us when we believed the parchment to be authentic, declined to go.

On close examination, it was not the same parchment as the forgery presented to us by Charles and Joseph, but it had similar content. We were amazed to find out many—but not all—of the flaws we discovered were absent. This parchment was clearly a second attempt and a much better one.

The museum director was far from pleased. With his gracious permission, we collected all the information we could about this strange forgery and its creators.

In addition to Charles Tock and Joseph, the director mentioned another man had been among those who had sold the parchment to the museum. The group went by different names, but a quick description of their physical attributes and mannerisms left little doubt as to the identity of two of the forgers. The third man—unknown to us—added to the mystery.

About the same time, one of our number discovered an advertisement in the prestigious Journal of Antiquity. A New York book dealer was offering a parchment from the Book of Jasher to "some museum or lover of the classical Biblical world" for four hundred dollars.

Taking an extended absence from our responsibilities, Christopher and I made the two hundred mile journey by rail and stagecoach and met the man. He had, of course, bought the parchment from Charles, Joseph, and the third man, again under false names. Once more, we discovered a clever forgery that showed a marked improvement in skill on the part of the forgers. I dare say, an expert not having been privy of the previous attempts would have been fooled.

Charles Tock had considerable talent and the knowledge needed, but we wondered whether he alone could have created the forgeries. They were, after all, marvelous in design and, while skilled in modern languages, Charles was not known to be a biblical language scholar. Joseph did not leave the impression of being a scholar at all, and we therefore surmised this third man, whoever he may be, must have possessed the requisite talent in this regard.

I then realized the whole matter if left unchecked would

blur the lines between truth and falsehood. Through books and articles, these forgeries had the power to influence scholarship for years to come. The criminals had to be stopped and we, experts in our fields, were best suited to complete the task.

Back at our weekly club meeting, I suggested our society should direct all its collective energies and talents into bringing the rogues to justice. We all were in agreement, except Thomas—who, at the time I assumed, was ashamed of his impetuous rush to authenticate the parchment and simply wanted to put the matter behind him. However, we could not tolerate deliberate falsehoods. With Charles Tock having been one of our members, we all felt a tinge of responsibility.

Immediately, our club journeyed to every museum and antiquities dealer or collector within a hundred-mile radius. We sent letters warning museums far and wide about the *Book of Jasher* forgeries. We took out advertisements in every journal and newspaper in the region. In all, our group invested hundreds of hours and dollars into the project.

After a few weeks, we ceased our efforts, convinced we had done our part to warn the public.

Unfortunately, this was only the beginning of the affair.

Once again, Charles reappeared just as suddenly as he had disappeared, but not in a way any of us would have wished.

It was the night of October 24th, 1859.

As it happened, I was on key duty that month, which meant I was to arrive early to open the meeting room and leave late to lock up.

As was required of me, I showed up early to unlock the room and prepare for the meeting. Thomas Phillips—who was known to be punctual but never early—was at the door, waiting for me.

"Carl, how are you this evening?"

"Fine. Fine. Shall we enter?"

I proceeded to open the premises and walk inside. Hearing a creaking, I looked up and in the stale light seeping through the curtained windows, I saw Charles hanging from the rafters, dead. His corpse swung slightly, and on his chest, I noticed someone had attached a note.

Thomas rushed to the body, steadied the swinging, and snatched the note.

"Carl, it simply reads, 'Two Tocks Before Midnight.'"

With no footstool beneath the body, we quickly determined, to our horror, a crime had been committed. This was no suicide. Someone had murdered Charles Tock.

CHAPTER FIVE

THE POLICE DID NOT TAKE LONG TO REACH THE PREMISES. Fellow members poured in, each wearing concerned and stern faces, as we explained the situation to them. Immediately, we all suspected the mug who had accompanied Charles the night of the parchment: Joseph.

To the best of our abilities, we each described him to the police detective, Captain Barnwell.

If you will forgive the momentary digression of an old man, Captain Barnwell became a close friend of the Society and it behooves me to take some time to describe the fellow.

Tall and ruddy in the face, he showed great aptitude in both his mental and physical faculties. His appearance seemed more of an athlete than a police captain, but this man with the body of a sprinter housed the mind of a quick-witted scholar.

During the length of our acquaintance, Captain Barnwell wore a large mustache which effectively masked his emotional state as well as his upper lip. One could never be certain the cards the captain held until he laid them on the table and the ends of his mustache wiggled accordingly.

You may never find a man with greater contrasting qualities. He was reticent to a fault regarding the social graces, but when the topic of crime arose, he shared his opinions with shocking celerity. Of popular literature and theater, he knew nothing and cared even less, but of the latest scientific discoveries—especially such as showing promise for use in deterring criminal activity—he was well versed.

I made mention of his mustache and to his mustache, I must return for it was his greatest detecting tool. During the questioning of a suspect, no matter how tight-lipped the man may have been, any falsehood or irrelevant fact was greeted with a twitching of his facial hair and with it, a most deprecating frown, from which few questioners could maintain deceipt. In numerous examples through the two decades of our friendship, I saw that man with his mustache wiggle out the truth in the most amazing ways.

Captain Barnwell leveled his mustache and applied his business-like eyes to some notes in his hand; his words, however, were directed to me. "You say this Joseph fellow seemed belligerent and treated Mr. Tock roughly?"

"Yes, that is correct," I answered. "In addition, two of the purchasers of a parchment mentioned a third man. We have no idea who he is, but he could have been the mastermind behind the forgeries and perhaps this." I pointed to the body which lay upon a canvas sheet on the floor.

"Two Tocks Before Midnight," said the captain. "What the devil could that mean? Charles' last name, of course, was Tock. Could it mean one of his relatives?"

After a quick consultation with the others, I spoke up. "We have never met any of his relations. He kept to himself and never spoke of anyone to go home to."

"Before midnight," said Christopher. "Wouldn't that imply that something will occur *tonight* by midnight? Could 'Two

Tocks' mean, 'two deaths like Tock' and these deaths would occur shortly before midnight tonight?"

It seemed a sensible interpretation. If so, we had less than six hours to prepare.

The group grew silent. And then, after some discussion, we decided, in the interest of safety, that all members would spend the night in the society room. Those with family were encouraged to bring their loved ones or take them to a place of shelter. Whoever the murderer happened to be, he was able to freely enter the club room where we stored the records and addresses of members.

I then remembered that over the years Charles had been with us, he had only recommended one fellow to join our ranks. We'd had no objections and he was quickly ushered in. That fellow was Thomas Phillips, the very same man who had entered the room with me and had co-discovered the body.

I searched for Thomas but could not find him. I further remembered he had been the only member to be overly eager to certify the authenticity of the parchment before it could be properly examined.

"Christopher," I waved until I raised his attention, "a word, please."

We huddled in a corner as I expressed my concerns. We both commented on how quiet he had been and we speculated that he might actually be a relative of Charles. If so, his life could be in danger.

We called the others and caught the captain before he left. As with Charles, it turned out the society records had a false address for Thomas: 114 Elm Street. One of our members lived nearby and assured us Elm Street only reached number 110.

Someone remembered seeing him at a bank as a teller. By this time, the clock had struck six, but we managed to track down the bank's manager who, after much pleading, opened the bank and gave us the address on file for Thomas. The address given was the same: 114 Elm Street.

Thomas had been introduced by Charles, and like Charles, he had given us a false address. He arrived early to be the first to discover Charles' body and then had promptly disappeared. All evidence seemed to indicate he was part of the plot. But was he the murderer or now a target—the second *Tock*?

Concerned, I considered the encounter with the body of Charles. It had been swinging slightly. Perhaps, the murder had just occurred. With further consideration, all doubt fled my mind. Charles must have died mere minutes prior to our entering the room. When cutting Charles down, the corpse had been warm. Thomas had been there before me and in my memory he had been in a state of agitation. He could have retained a key to the room. He could have entered with Charles and murdered him there. It seemed the most likely explanation as I had seen no one else in the area.

By eleven o'clock, we had regrouped and all members waited in the club meeting room. Thomas was still absent as were a few other members—mostly those with families.

Due to the extraordinary situation, the fact the killer potentially had studied our personal addresses, and the specific time given for the promised crime, Captain Barnwell dispatched officers to each of our houses to watch the homes. We warned the police that Thomas was an expert with weaponry and may be armed.

Christopher pulled me aside. "Do you not remember the key passage from the parchment? '...only teach thy sons the use of the bow and all weapons of war.'"

"Yes. The bow. Thomas once spoke of his collection and how he enjoyed hunting with nothing more than a bow and a quiver full of arrows."

Christopher talked to the others about our little theory while I searched the room. We had but two links to the outside: the door and a single window. We were on the second floor over an antique bookseller's shop. The window would only be a danger if a shooter were to be located in the apartments across the street.

The door was constantly opening and shutting even at that late hour—far too many people were coming and going bringing in family members or looking outside. The police were also entering and leaving, asking for more information about Thomas. I realized we needed the door locked with everyone inside immediately.

Then, a thought caused my frame to shiver: the killer had entered through the locked door once before.

"Barricade the door and stand clear of the window!" I shouted to everyone's alarm.

Before my instructions could lead to action, at precisely half an hour before midnight, Thomas reappeared.

Conversation ceased, and all heads turned to face him.

"I do apologize for my late arrival." Clearly seeing he had everyone's total attention, he continued, "I wanted to arrive earlier, but I had to make sure my property was secure." He explained he had run into his landlady and the encounter had delayed him further.

I approached Thomas to confront him.

"Are you a relative of Charles?"

Thomas seemed almost hurt by the accusation.

"What?"

"You gave a false address to the club. 114 Elm Street does not exist."

"You are mistaken. It does exist. That is my mother's address in Chelsea. When I began here, I was living there."

I was taken aback by his quick reply. It did not seem to be a forced answer to cover a lie.

He walked to the middle of the room. "My dear fellows. You suspect me of being involved with those rogues? Yes, I was excited when I thought the parchment was true, but weren't we all?" No one said a word, but everyone listened intently. "I suggest we do not point fingers. 'Two Tocks Before Midnight' it said. We have but thirty minutes to discover whether the whole message is nothing but a trick. Then, with clear minds, we shall discover who is behind all this business." He shook his head. "I assure you, it wasn't me."

Nearly everyone flooded to Thomas with the sincerest of apologies. I decided to wait until after midnight to offer mine. It was a clever retort, but I was yet to be convinced Thomas had no part in the affair.

"Everyone, listen," I said after giving Thomas a few minutes. "We have precious little time until midnight. We need to bar the door and stand clear from the window."

"Please excuse me for being rude," Thomas shouted, turning everyone's attention from me to him, "but after you falsely accused me of being a murderer, do you really think we should take orders from you? Lock the door, indeed, but what is with the window? Do you expect the angel of death to fly through on the stroke of midnight?"

He had moved in front of the window, taunting and strutting as a peacock for the attention of the others.

Thomas was emotionally upset—as would I, had I been accused of murder unjustly. But if he truly was the murderer, the truth had to be fleshed out before another could be killed.

I was preparing myself to explain our theory about the killer using a bow through the window when exactly the same occurred.

I can still recall the horror of that moment. Even now, it causes me to flinch. The shards of glass flew, but did no damage. The bolt, however, pierced Thomas' right arm, taking shirt cloth and skin alike until the projectile landed with a thud in the far wall. The collective gasps of the people in the room gave way to the sound of footfalls as everyone moved as far from the window as the room permitted.

Thomas dropped to the ground and I immediately rushed to him, keeping below the window. The wound, however superficial, was a testament to all that I had wrongly accused an innocent man.

Still, being near the window, I distinctly heard, from the outside, a piece of wood cracking and then a soft thud onto the street below.

"Listen!" I yelled, somewhat calming the commotion.

"I heard it too," said the captain. "Follow me."

Leaving others to attend to the stricken man, I pushed all emotions and bubbling guilt aside and rushed out the door, following Captain Barnwell and two police officers down the stairs. The killer was outside and a mere matter of seconds could mean his capture or escape.

Captain Barnwell held the lamp ahead of us, but even with the light we almost tripped over the body.

Joseph.

By the look of it, Joseph had taken the shot with the bow and had then fallen the two stories to his death. We found a crossbow, scattered bolts, and broken pieces of wood within a few feet from the body.

Looking up, we saw the balcony from the second floor had missing boards. Joseph had simply applied too much of his heavy frame to it.

But it was curious in that I heard only a single crack of wood and a soft thud. I heard no scream. I saw no one pouring out from the building awakened by the noise. It was instantly apparent to me that something was wrong with the scene.

The captain, worked his lantern over the length of the corpse.

"Captain," I said, gaining his attention, "there remains one more. The third man. He most certainly is still in the vicinity."

"Quite right," Captain Barnwell said, kneeling beside the body and playing his clinical eyes over it in search of clues."In that case, it may be better to search the area. You should return and leave the police work to us. It could be dangerous."

"If it is all the same with you," I said, revealing a pistol I had hidden inside my coat pocket, "I am very interested in what we find upstairs. I suspect we will discover the plot behind all these devilish deeds."

"I wouldn't think we will find much up there. Whoever the third man is wouldn't be so foolish as to stay at the exact spot of the crime."

"I'm not expecting a person, Captain. I'm expecting a candle."

"A candle, sir?"

I had caught the slightest whiff of melted wax and burnt wick. It brought to my memory an old time-delaying trick I'd learned during a brief stint in Europe.

The apartment building stood four stories high. The room we wanted was on the second floor. We woke the apartment manager and, after explaining our requirements, he quickly dressed himself and led us upstairs.

The room was let to an elderly woman who rarely left her apartment. Fearing the worst, the manager used his key after the third series of knocks.

Our fears were brutally justified.

"No doubt the old woman surprised the man as he was heading for the balcony."

"The men, you mean, Captain."

"The men, sir?"

"Shall we head to the balcony?" I said, not wanting to reveal my suspicions without further data.

The frail balcony door had been left open. We could see the broken railing and across the street, a perfect view of our meeting place.

"A moment, please," I said, borrowing the captain's lantern and kneeling at the balcony threshold. I examined the area, careful to illuminate every inch. The balcony was small; perhaps only two men standing shoulder to shoulder could fit.

As I suspected, there was indeed a hardened puddle of white wax in front of a knocked over piece of wood.

Carefully leaning over, I retrieved a small nail from the corner. Next, I rose and stepped out onto the balcony to examine the remnants of the railing. The wood was indeed old and weak, but not rotted. To me, the lone nail and the lack of rot indicated a saboteur.

Holding up the nail for the captain to take, I said, "If we find the boards downstairs with holes but no nails, we have 'men,' not 'man.'"

"The third man."

"Yes," I replied.

"But why?"

"Which 'why'? There is a big why and a small why. The big why, the reason for all this, is a mystery to me. But the small why, the reason for the unmanned launch, is to create an alibi."

"Do you suspect... Thomas?"

"I do, sir."

"Mr. Brooke, if you are correct and, I must say I believe you may very well be, you've made my job much easier. However, the law requires direct evidence. All we have is circumstantial." He paused before adding, "Are you in the mood for a spot of acting?"

"'All the world's a stage,' so sayeth the Bard. What do you have in mind?"

"Let's tell the truth… up to a point. I believe, there was a witness, wouldn't you agree?" said the captain with a wink.

"Quite."

CHAPTER SIX

Captain Barnwell and I returned to the group. He asked his two officers to fetch some materials from the department and wait outside the door.

Everyone was silent and seated, eager to hear our report. Thomas had a new smug look on his face. In retrospect, I believe it had always been there, but the new information had simply opened my eyes to it.

The captain raised his hands to gather the attention that was already his. My eyes fixed on Thomas throughout Captain Barnwell's speech.

"Joseph is dead. Mr. Brooke here has confirmed his identity."

My friends took a moment to let out a "thank God" or "a fitting ending to this horrible affair."

"Sirs, that is not all."

The men ceased their chatter and again gave the captain their undivided attention. Thomas remained the very definition of confidence.

"An elderly woman was killed tonight."

"By Joseph?" asked Christopher.

"Perhaps," the captain said with dramatic pause, "...or Joseph's murderer."

Expressions turned from a pitiful concern for the elderly woman to confusion. It was assumed by all that Joseph's death had been accidental. The nearly imperceptible smile that I alone had noticed on Thomas' lips disappeared.

"Joseph's murderer? Could this be the third man?" asked someone.

"That is our belief," answered the captain. "While we do not yet have the man's identity, we do have a witness."

I am sure the captain paused to allow me to closely examine Thomas' reaction to the word, "witness." His face was stale, motionless. Had I not observed his earlier smugness, I would have had to say his face registered no reaction. But it did; I saw the slight change in his disposition. And with that change, I saw guilt.

The captain continued, "A neighbor saw a mustached stranger wearing a dark coat enter the room across the street," He pointed in the direction of the old woman's apartment. "She got a good look at the man's profile. The witness is in police custody and we will shortly have a drawing done revealing the murderer."

The chatter began anew. Thomas, the only man in the room with a mustache, stood and began moving toward the door.

"I'm terribly sorry," the captain said restraining Thomas with his arm but speaking to everyone, "but in the interest of your safety and police procedure, I must ask for each of you to remain here until the drawing can be completed. It is a dreadful inconvenience, but essential to our case. It is possible—indeed, probable—that one of you may know the man's identity and the whole matter will be brought to a happy conclusion tonight."

Thomas seemed to be on the verge of becoming belligerent, but after a moment, he reposed himself and returned to his seat next to the window without complaint.

"The department is a mere five-minute walk from here. The drawing should be here momentarily."

That is what he told our group, but in actuality, the captain had told his officers to wait outside for a full hour before entering with a satchel containing a blank sheet of drawing paper.

Minutes passed. Most members seemed to enjoy the waiting as if watching the lead-up to the climax of some exciting play.

And so it was—the captain's play.

Thomas, however, seemed more and more troubled. I no longer stared at him directly, but even a casual glance told me he understood the game we were playing.

The clock against the wall was near Thomas. Its tick-tock seemed to unnerve him more. Did its sound remind him of the two Tocks?

I will summarize that hour with the following description: most members were amiable despite having no knowledge of our drama. Toward the end, however, a few began to tire of conversation and wished to return home no matter the risk. Thomas took the opportunity to speak up.

"This is intolerable. You cannot keep us here like rats in some insane experiment," he said, standing.

"An interesting metaphor, Thomas," I said, seeing my opportunity. "An experiment expects some result. What kind of result do you expect?"

He was quiet. Sweat formed on his forehead, although it was not at all warm that October evening. There was no doubt then; he was guilty, and we had him.

"You are, of course, expecting your face on the paper."

"Oh, come now old boy," began one member in defense of

Thomas. "Do let's put all this aside. Haven't you had enough fun at Thomas' expense today?"

"But," the captain said, raising his hand effectively silencing the entire room. "What if the accusation is true? After all, he wears a mustache."

The room was ablaze with discussion, half of the room watched Thomas, the other half looked on me.

Thomas was shaking slightly when the knock to the door silenced the room once more. The officer walked in and after shooting a stern glance in Thomas' direction, he handed the satchel to the captain. The captain opened the bag and pulled the sheet of paper half-way out with an ostentatious display. With slow, deliberate motions, he returned the paper to the satchel, looked directly at Thomas, and cleared his throat.

"There can be little doubt, now." The captain's mustache remained motionless, forming the picture of a man with complete control of his being.

"There was no witness!" Thomas shouted.

"How could you know?" I retorted. "Unless, of course, you were there."

"I was here, you fool. I was here when the dart was shot, when Joseph fell to his death!"

"The dart, yes. Joseph's death, no," I said, taking a step toward Thomas.

"But Thomas was shot by an arrow," someone replied, rallying to Thomas' defense. "Someone who went to the trouble to create his own alibi would have no reason to risk being killed."

"Thomas is an expert marksman. He knew exactly where to stand in order to not hit his vital organs," I explained, keeping my eyes burning on Thomas. "But you were not intending to even graze yourself, were you? When you came inside around 11:30, there was no wind. I conferred with a policeman who had been stationed outside at the time. You aimed the crossbow precisely on target without correcting for wind. At 11:45 when the arrow was fired, however, there was a slight western wind, pulling the arrow to the left. You had intended it to come close, but not touch."

"But," someone else said, "how on earth could he have fired a crossbow across the street while physically standing here?"

"He used a candle as a fuse. He lit the candle shortly before 11:30. It burned for fifteen minutes at which point, the wick set off the main fuse which released a weight pulling the trigger. The kickback from the launched arrow pulled the last nail causing the already dead Joseph, crossbow, and rock to fall to the ground. With the poor light outside, the thread you used to tie the rock is practically invisible. Not knowing what to look for, the police wouldn't have bothered with one of a hundred rocks on the street. You intended to retrieve this on your way home, hadn't you?" I said, pulling out the rock and dangling it from a two-foot length of twine held by my fingers.

"But if he used a candle, surely we would have seen its light?" This time, Christopher spoke up.

"The crossbow was set on a piece of wood on the edge of the balcony. The candle was behind that wood, shielding its light from our view."

"You are insane," said Thomas in a fit of rage.

No one spoke in his defense.

"But the look of surprise on your face when the arrow flew into the window was not feigned," I said, addressing Thomas directly. "Oh, no. You were not expecting the shot so soon. Again, the wind worked against your wishes. Instead of twenty minutes, the candle, being fed extra airflow, burned the fuse in fewer than fifteen!"

All eyes were on Thomas who was now silent, clearly considering his options.

"I have to admit, it was ingenious," I continued in a softer tone. "Had I not witnessed a candle fuse before among miners in Southern France, I would have glossed over the slight remnants of wax on the balcony."

"You have no proof."

"Do you remember," I said, taking a step toward the murdering savage, "when Joseph returned to retrieve the parchment and we told him it was a forgery? We told Joseph nothing of our reasons. And yet, the parchment we found at the Chelsea museum corrected the Hebrew and stylistic issues. The exact issues we as a group spoke of only among ourselves."

"Surely Charles heard—"

"No," I said sternly, anticipating his words. "Charles was not there. He only returned to us this evening, hanging from a rope."

"You still have no proof," he said almost in a scream.

"We have a witness."

Thomas whipped out a pistol; I pulled out mine. The captain and the policeman beside him also had their service pistols drawn. The other members huddled, gasping at the unexpected development.

"But I must ask," I said as calmly as possible. "Why all this? What purpose did all these deaths serve?" Memory recalls my voice much steadier than how it really was.

Thomas kept silent but his gun remained steady.

"There was money at stake, of course, but there was something else, wasn't there? Something personal," I said, trying to read meaning from his expression.

"Who was Joseph?" asked the captain.

"You don't know by now?" Thomas answered, anger clear in his intonation. "Charles Tock's half-brother of course. He was an idiot, but Charles pampered him to his own hurt, blinded by some sense of loyalty to the dumb beast."

Thomas became talkative.

"Come, let us sit down at the station and have a long talk," said Captain Barnwell, edging closer to the increasingly desperate man.

Thomas backed up against the window, shards of glass surely pricking his back.

"All right. I'm giving up," he said, showing the broadside of his gun. But just as he appeared to lower it, he threw the pistol with a great force across the room. Instinctively my eyes followed the flight of the pistol. Turning back to Thomas, I watched as he leapt out the broken window.

We all rushed to see him roll off an awning and fall into the street.

"Quick! Downstairs!"

The men followed the police downstairs, breathlessly expecting a fourth body for the night. But reaching the location mere seconds after Thomas had jumped, we found no body. Bits of bloodied glass and wood fragments lay scattered on the cobbles, but no Thomas.

The street, at that time, was poorly lit. Even with the lantern the captain carried, the fiend had ample shadows in which to hide. We scoured the neighborhood but found… nothing.

CHAPTER SEVEN

IN THE MORNING'S LIGHT, MINUTE TRAILS OF BLOOD LED US TO believe our fugitive had entered the apartment building across from our meeting hall. Somehow, the bloodied mess of a man had crept inside while we were all flying down the stairs.

A door to door search revealed his hiding place. By morning, he had vanished, but the occupant, a middle-aged woman living alone, was tied and gagged. We had expected the worst, but he had left her alive. She had watched, bound, as he mended his wounds and left before the sun broke through the mist.

NEITHER THE POLICE nor the *Agora Society* ever found Thomas. The search for the missing killer would remain a pet project that would pester Captain Barnwell until the day he died some ten years ago.

But stranger still, every year, on October 24th, I have, without fail, received a curious card in my mailbox. The card always arrived with but one word on it.

The first year—the first anniversary—I received the card, it read, "Tick." I discarded it as some nonsensical childish prank without even considering the date. However, the second year, the card read, "Tock," and I was terrified. Of all the *Agora* members, I had been most integral in discovering Thomas' hand in the matter. Captain Barnwell had a man stay at my house for the following week.

Of course, nothing ever happened. Except for the card alternating between "Tick" and "Tock" every year, I never saw or heard from Thomas again.

A few times I stayed vigil all night watching for him to insert the card. I learned he used delivery boys to leave the cards, never exposing himself directly. I always interrogated the boys—a different one each year—but they all said the same thing: the benefactor was a stranger. A tall man with a scarred face. And they were all paid handsomely for the delivery. Investigating the location the boys gave presented no clues and no Thomas. Ever.

The cards came religiously every year on October 24th. Every year until last year... It now being November of the following year, I feel that I truly am the last of the *Agora Society*.

THE MYSTERY HAS ONLY RECENTLY BEEN MADE manifest. Shortly after writing the above, a woman named Lottie Phillips visited me in my lodgings. In her mid-thirties, she was a charming woman, well-spoken and regally dressed. She presented to me a letter sealed and addressed with my name, care of the Agora Society.

She discovered the letter after her father's death. Being curious, she traveled from Georgia to deliver it herself, hoping to learn something of her father's mysterious past. The contents of the letter revealed her to be Thomas Phillips' daughter. I then realized that Thomas had taken his wife down south to hide from the law. As befitting a lady of honor, she did not open the letter nor did she demand I read the contents aloud.

THE LETTER READS AS FOLLOWS:

My Dear Carl,

By receipt of this post, you have evidence that Thomas Phillips is dead. What I did after the Agora Society is irrelevant and by offering you this information, I only ask you not disturb my family.

I became acquainted with Charles through the bank of my employment. And from that acquaintance, I was introduced to the Agora Society, his brother Joseph, and most importantly his daughter Carolyn.

I soon discovered Joseph's lust for money. Charles's brother was stupid and a petty thief, but I must admit, the forgeries were his idea. Upon seeing the blank parchments that Charles had acquired during one of his travels, Joseph asked of their value and from there the idea of the Book of Jasher *forgeries was born.*

We began work on our scheme a full year before the events of that horrid October. To keep our secret intact, Charles and I rarely spoke to each other at the Agora and never spoke of our families or social activities.

Emotional attachments are so often the downfall of great enterprises and so it was with ours.

I asked Charles for his daughter's hand in marriage. Carolyn and I had already pledged our love and needed only her father's permission.

But it was not to be.

He was furious and resolute against the idea of giving his daughter to a criminal as he called me. He would have broken off all contact with me had we not had the shared guilt of the forgeries together.

A few months later, Carolyn and I secretly eloped and moved across town. I still kept residence at my old place to receive visitors and of course to meet with Charles and Joseph, but at night, I flew to Carolyn. Her father, who did not know her whereabouts, was distraught.

We planned to move to a new town and leave it all behind, eventually sending Charles a letter explaining our marriage. I even gave notice to the bank. During that time, we were careful not to expose our location to anyone who knew her father. I double-backed and made false turns to thwart onlookers from learning of our location. Carolyn even wore heavy scarves around her head as disguise.

But Joseph found us.

He threatened to tell Charles of our marriage and to tell Carolyn about our nefarious activities—the facts of which she was never made privy.

Charles of course was in despair. He had no idea what had become of Carolyn and assumed the worst. He contacted the police and posted bulletins describing her appearance. Charles then quit the Agora Society and plunged completely into what he was best at: creating the forgeries. And so, the three of us, encouraged by Charles' determination, redoubled our efforts.

Again, it was Joseph's idea to approach the Agora Society in hopes the experts there would certify the authenticity of the parchment. Such an endorsement would surely have enabled us to fetch ten times the amount we were seeking.

The Book of Jasher *became Charles' sole reason for living. If you remember that night he appeared with the* parchment, his nervousness prevented him from going back to hear your conclusion.

As you so keenly surmised, I instructed them according to the points you made clear and, together, the three of us created and sold corrected parchments for a tidy profit.

If it were not for your insistence, our little endeavor would have succeeded without harm. But after reading your advertisement, Charles felt we could not continue. While strong in intellectual matters, he was exceedingly weak in will.

One day, standing before Joseph and me, he declared his intent to confess the whole matter. Clearly, this was not acceptable to Joseph or myself. To have such a blight against my name was unthinkable. For Joseph, the reasons were purely financial.

We tried to stop Charles, but he was most insistent.

It was Joseph's idea to kill his relative and to have the body discovered at the Agora Society. I argued against it, but Joseph again threatened to reveal our activities to Carolyn if I didn't go along. I relented after devising a way to rid myself of both Tocks so Carolyn and I could begin our marriage properly. It required both Joseph's strength and... his death.

It turned out the Agora for the location was a good idea—and would have worked, I am sure, had you not been there. Joseph would be a natural suspect among any of you. Hence, the decision to stage the hanging at the Agora was perfect. When Joseph, the perceived murderer, died attempting to murder me, no one with any knowledge of our activities would remain alive. And with me being among the victims, no one would suspect me of the crime.

At least, that was my plan.

But back to that night.

The fool Charles had fled to the Agora Society no doubt with a mind to confess to you all that evening. For us, to find him outside the doors waiting for you to open it, was fortuitous.

Of course, I had made a copy of the key from when I was on key duty and had easy access to the room. From there, with big Joseph's help, it was an easy matter to subdue and hang Charles.

You may wonder about Joseph. He was indeed Charles' half-brother, but with Charles threatening to end the easy income, jealousy overruled reason. Charles was the favored child—for his well-formed brain and the fact that Joseph was born a bastard. Joseph hated his brother with passion and only tolerated him thus far for his money-making potential. With that gone, Joseph preferred to see Charles dead. Dead men can name no names.

Regarding this, I was in happy agreement with Joseph, but Joseph likewise, had too much knowledge of our enterprise. More importantly, there was the matter of blackmail.

While Joseph did much of the work as I commanded, he did not know the end of my plot. He asked why the candles. I softly replied, "You'll see." But now I realize I had lied. He never would see.

You may wonder why I have not sought revenge against you. After all, you are responsible for me losing a great deal of money. I should also mention the fact that you are responsible for the deaths of three persons.

In truth, I had intended to seek revenge, slowly. I wanted the "Tick Tock" letters to strike fear into you before I pounced. I planned an elaborate setup far more advanced than that of October 24th, 1859. But as time passed, my passion ebbed, my business increased, and most importantly, Carolyn and I had a child. Eventually, I lost all zeal in the matter. I did continue the yearly cards out of tradition and nostalgia, however. I do hope you enjoyed my efforts.

You may further wonder why I write this. I shall never

*post this letter while alive, but in lieu of a confession, this
enables me to offer you—should you outlive me—a more
complete account of that evening.*

Your Obedient Servant,
    TP

---

* * *

Having no hand or knowledge in the affairs of her father,
I felt it best to let Lottie Phillips live her life without
knowing her father's darker side. I told her nothing of the
contents of the letter, but spent the time, instead, telling her
stories of her father before that dreadful night, before he
murdered her grandfather and uncle.

After she left, I realized Thomas had given his daughter a
name cognate with "Charles" as well as my name, "Carl."
Lottie is a pet form of Charlotte, which is also related to
churl. I spent that night in thought. Was the name given out
of respect or guilt? Perhaps some attempt at penitence? Or
was it simple coincidence?

So THERE, the matter is resolved, and the world has the full
story. Having only learned much of it recently myself, I feel
somewhat relieved, completed.

Ironically, although Thomas had intended to tear the
Agora Society apart, his actions had quite the opposite effect.
We gained some measure of fame due to the incident, and
many of our members went on to great worldly success.

The redoubtable Captain Barnwell often visited as a
welcomed guest. He would present particularly troublesome

cases for the club to consider, and, as a group, our members became closer than family.

With respect to our society, Thomas failed completely. But regarding his motivation behind it all, Carolyn, he most definitely succeeded.

Love can lead some men to greatness, others to their downfall. They say love triumphs over evil, but for Thomas, it only amplified the darkness that lay within him. Lies. Jealousy. Death. This was the legacy of Thomas and his "Two Tocks Before Midnight," the first great case of the *Agora Society*.

CONTINUE READING

Did you enjoy Two Tocks? Do you like reading of murder, mayhem, and the gentleman detective?

If so, look for The Agora Letters Volume 1 **includes five full-length stories** for one low price.

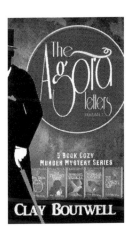

In the style of Arthur Conan Doyle, Clay Boutwell brings back the Agora Society and its premiere scholar, Carl Brooke.

A string of thefts ends in a grisly murder. Certain evidence leads Captain Barnwell to suspect a former thief, Rutherford Nordlinger as the culprit. Carl Brooke becomes personally involved as Nordlinger's guilt is questioned.

"My hands instinctively gripped my knees and I bowed my head down to the carriage floor. It was pure shock, those words."

Buy The Agora Letters Volume 1 which includes five stories (including The Penitent Thief, The Peace Party Massacre, The Curse of the Mad Sheik, and The Captain's Play) for the price of three.

THE HANDKERCHIEF, A SHORT STORY

My wife was to come in on the last flight of the night. She had been staying with her sister saying she needed "her space." I had a feeling this time around, she had returned only to collect her things.

Having found a plug just outside the terminal parking lot, I decided to charge my laptop and work on a spreadsheet before heading in. It had been a long day at the office and finding a plug in a secluded and lonely place seemed fortuitous.

I hunkered down in a darkish corner as travelers went from cars to planes and back again. Fascinated by the faces of the hurried people, I abandoned my spreadsheet, eventually closing the laptop completely.

No doubt, anyone would have noticed me staring if they had simply turned to look, but no one did. My dark suit and the poor lighting helped, but I think it was something else: for most, destinations and goals are all there is.

For most, but not all.

I had never seen such sadness. The boy was flying out and the girl was there to see him off. He was decked out in full uniform with a duffel bag at his feet; she wore a flowery summer dress much too happy for their despondent quality. Her bright lipstick was somehow dulled by the sadness in her eyes. Neither, it seemed, had the courage to say, "Good-bye."

He lifted his hands to caress her cheeks. For a moment, I thought he was about to kiss her, but his eyes revealed a man busy memorizing his lover's features. Every shape and line, it all had meaning.

A tinny speaker announced that boarding had begun. The message didn't seem to register until he let his arms drop. Her eyes puffed red as tears began to swell.

He pulled out a handkerchief–it was pale, green army issue. She wiped both eyes before kissing it, imparting both lipstick and tears to the cloth. Handing it back, he accepted it, his eyes never leaving hers.

She mouthed some unknown words, turned, and then fled toward the parking lot with her head buried in her hands.

His military posture slumped as she disappeared into the darkness. The handkerchief, he lovingly folded and placed in the side pocket of his duffle bag.

It was the speaker again–this time announcing final boarding. In a hurried motion, he snapped his hand from the side pocket unknowingly exposing the cherished cloth. With a flick of his wrist, he threw the bag over his shoulder. A moment later, the man was gone; only the handkerchief remained.

I sat there stunned, unable to move, minutes passing. Coming to my senses, my first thought was to rush to the fallen handkerchief and find that soldier who by then was long gone.

But as my thoughts began to translate into action, a green vested airport worker appeared where the forlorn lovers had been. She held metal tongs as if the precious article was hazardous material. A moment later, the lipstick, tears, and cloth were gone.

Rarely do emotions get the better of me. But after packing my laptop, I headed straight to the airport gift shop. The flowers made my wife smile–the first time in years.

And now, ten years later, I still buy flowers and she still smiles. I can say it was because of that handkerchief–a handkerchief long forgotten by all but me.

WANT A FREE EBOOK?

Head over to www.ClayBoutwell.com for fiction and/or www.TheJapanShop.com for Japanese instructional books. FREE!

Clay Boutwell and his wife Yumi are the authors of several top ten books on learning Japanese, including: Hiragana, the Basics of Japanese, and Hikoichi, the first in their Japanese Reader Collection series. They have over twenty titles and are slowly adding more readers and study guides as ebooks and paperbacks. And...EVERY purchase comes with FREE MP3s!

His fiction includes thrillers (Tanaka and the Yakuza's Daughter), mysteries (Two Tocks before Midnight), and, yes, superheroes! (The Temporal)

www.ClayBoutwell.com
   www.TheJapanShop.com
   www.TheJapanesePage.com

Please contact the author at clay@clayboutwell.com or visit his blog at: http://www.ClayBoutwell.com
Your comments and questions are most welcome.

Printed in Great Britain
by Amazon